Twelfth Night

Retold by Sue Purkiss

Illustrated by Serena Curmi

A & C Black • London

First published 2010 by
A & C Black Publishers Ltd
36 Soho Square, London, W1D 3QY

www.acblack.com

ISBN 978-1-4081-1054-6

A CIP catalogue for this book is available from the British Library.

Printed and bound in Great Britain
by CPI Cox & Wyman, Reading, RG1 8EX.

Contents

List of characters

Orsino, *Duke of Illyria*

Sebastian, *brother of Viola*

Antonio, *a sea captain, friend to Sebastian*

Viola, *sister of Sebastian*

Olivia, *a rich countess*

Sir Toby Belch, *uncle of Olivia*

Sir Andrew Aguecheek

Malvolio, *steward to Olivia*

Fabian, *servant to Olivia*

Feste, *servant to Olivia, a clown*

Maria, *Olivia's lady-in-waiting*

Curio, *attendant to the duke*

Valentine, *attendant to the duke*

A sea captain, *friend to Viola*

Two officers of the law

A priest

Act One

Welcome to Illyria, where our story takes place.

Do you know it? It's a small state in Italy, on the shores of the Mediterranean. The coast is charming and picturesque, but danger lies beneath the surface. Savage rocks lurk in the turquoise waters. Usually a gentle sun shines, but sometimes fierce storms blow up out of nowhere. Things aren't always what they seem, as many a sea captain has found out to his cost.

Illyria's ruler is the Duke Orsino. He's young, rich and handsome and, until recently, he was perfectly happy. Why wouldn't he be? He had everything he could possibly want. But then he fell for a girl called Olivia, and all that changed.

Orsino couldn't settle to anything. He prowled up and down the room, looking for something – anything – to take his mind off this marvellous girl who was driving him crazy. He noticed that the musicians had stopped playing and were looking at him expectantly.

'No, don't stop!' he said, running a hand through his hair till it stood up on end. 'If music be the food of love, give me excess of it... Perhaps it'll work like eating too much. It'll make me sick, and then that'll put me off – love, I mean, not food – and I'll be back to normal again. Excellent – there's a plan, let's try it! Go on – play, I tell you!'

The musicians glanced at each other, shrugged, and started up again. But after a few minutes, Orsino threw himself into a chair and groaned. 'No, stop! It's not working. Sorry, sorry, but it's just not.' He turned to his friend, who was idly strumming a lute, trying to play along with the professionals. 'Curio, what am I going to do? It's Olivia – I just can't stop thinking about her!'

'Er ... perhaps you'd like to go hunting, my lord? Take your mind off things?' Curio suggested helpfully.

Orsino sighed. 'It will take more than that,' he said. 'I'm the one who's being hunted.

Hounded by love...' His eyes lit up as another of his friends came in. 'Ah, Valentine – here you are at last. Tell me quickly – what did Olivia say? Has she changed her mind? Will she see me?'

Valentine shook his head apologetically. 'I'm sorry, my lord. Her maid says she's still in mourning for her brother. She's sworn to shut herself away for seven years. She won't see anyone at all, and certainly not a suitor. She's absolutely determined. She won't even think about love.'

'What? But that's ridiculous! Although...' Orsino brightened a little as a happy thought struck him. 'Just think, Valentine! If she feels this much for a brother, imagine how she'll feel when she does fall in love – which of course will be with me...'

On the coast, a few miles away, Viola's hair was tangled with salt, and her clothes were soaked. Tears ran down her face, but she didn't notice them. She stared out to sea, searching desperately for some sign that her brother might still be alive. The water was calm now, lapping gently at the beach. It was difficult to believe that last night a storm had whipped the waves into such a fury that their ship had been driven onto rocks and smashed to pieces. She had survived, rescued by the captain. He was standing beside her now, looking at her anxiously.

But for the moment she couldn't feel grateful, as she knew she should. She and her twin were orphans. Sebastian was everything to her. They were close as only twins can be, and now he was missing. She couldn't bear the thought that she lived while he had died, and she couldn't imagine how she would be able to live without him. She'd raced up and down the beach, turning over every bit of driftwood, every piece of wreckage. But search as she might, there was no trace of him.

Viola's shoulders sagged, and she turned

wearily to the captain. 'What country is this?' she asked.

'Illyria, my lady,' he answered. He glanced round at the curve of golden sand. The waves, gentle now, lapped at the beach, and his face softened. 'I know it well. As a matter of fact, I was born not far from here.'

Viola was hardly listening. 'Is there any chance?' she burst out. 'Is there any chance at all that he might have been saved?'

'It's possible,' said the captain. 'The last time I saw him, he was holding onto a piece of wood. Who knows? Perhaps he survived, just as we did. But we have searched all along the shore and he's nowhere to be found. My lady – what do you want to do?'

Viola was silent for a moment. Then, with an effort, she decided to pull herself together. She had survived. She had to make a choice. She could either give up and sit here weeping till she died, too, or decide what to do next. She made up her mind, and turned to the captain.

Her tears would have to wait.

'Tell me about this place,' she said. 'Who's in charge here?'

'The Duke Orsino, my lady,' said the captain.

'What kind of man is he? What's he like?'

'Well, he's not exactly a close personal friend,' said the captain, frowning. 'But from what I've heard, he's well thought of.' He chuckled. 'Actually, now I come to think of it, there was a story about him going round last time I was home, about a month ago.'

Viola waited.

'Well?' she said. 'What was this story?'

'Eh? Oh, they say he's fallen for the Lady Olivia.'

'And who's she?'

'Her father was a count. He died a year ago. The young lady was left in the care of her brother. But then, sad to say, he died, too. And the Lady Olivia was so upset, she declared that that was it.'

'That what was what?'

16

'Well, she said that since she'd lost the two men she loved most dearly in all the world, she wouldn't receive anybody or have anything to do with another man for seven whole years. So – not good news for Orsino.'

Viola sighed. 'Well, I can certainly understand how she feels. I'd like to crawl away and hide, too. But what she's doing is a little extreme.'

'Couldn't say, my lady.'

'No, of course you couldn't. But it is, all the same. And it's actually a bit inconvenient. I could have gone to her and asked for help. As it is...'

'Yes, my lady?'

'It's going to have to be the duke, isn't it? I'll tell you what – I have the beginnings of a plan. I'll dress up as a boy and go into the duke's service – you shall take me to his palace.' Viola paused. 'I've seen one of my brother's boxes on the shore. It's the one he kept his clothes in. I'll borrow some of them.' She was quiet for a moment. 'It'll make me feel a little closer to him as well… It's a good plan, I'm sure. There's nothing for me at home and, anyway, I'm not leaving here till I know for certain what's happened to Sebastian.'

The captain was startled. 'But … are you sure, my lady? Is there no other way?'

Viola sighed. 'Think about it. I can't just turn up as a lost girl, can I? At best he'll boss me about, and at worst … well, who knows what might happen? No, trust me, dear captain, this is the best plan – so you will help me, won't you?'

Her eyes were very large and very blue, and her lip trembled pitifully. The captain sighed. 'Whatever you say, my lady. Of course I will.'

Olivia had decided that her household was to live a life of quiet seclusion, in keeping with her grief over her brother's death. But not everyone was happy with the new regime. In particular, her uncle, Sir Toby Belch. Sir Toby had always enjoyed a drink – or two, or three – much more than the next man, and saw no reason why this should change. Maria, Olivia's lady-in-waiting, was trying to explain to him that his niece had had enough of his drunken antics.

'My lady has ordered me to tell you that she won't put up with you rolling in drunk at all hours. She's in mourning and she simply cannot cope with that kind of behaviour.'

Sir Toby tutted impatiently. 'Yes, yes, I know all that and it's very sad, but don't you think she's overdoing it a bit? Life must go on, after all. Life must go on!'

'She wasn't overly pleased about you bringing Sir Andrew Aguecheek to the house, either,' Maria went on. 'Especially when you told her what a fine husband he'd make.'

'Well, it's true. Agueface is a splendid fellow and a fine figure of a man. Just the job for her.'

'He's an idiot, he spends money hand over fist, and his ears stick out,' said Maria, who didn't believe in mincing her words. 'And you and he get drunk every night. She wouldn't touch him with a ten-foot barge pole.'

'So you don't think she's very keen, then?'
Sir Toby pondered. 'Oh dear, that's very
unfortunate. And here he comes, poor chap.
Not a word! If he realises he isn't in with a
chance, he might take umbrage and go – and
then what would I do for pocket money?'

Maria shook her head, made her excuses,
and left them to it. She had a soft spot for Sir
Toby, but really, there were times when he was
his own worst enemy.

Viola's plan had gone perfectly. Everyone
readily accepted who she was. She had arrived
at Orsino's court as a man, and it never
occurred to anyone to doubt her. Within a few
days, she was one of the duke's favourites. He
found her – Cesario, as she was now known –
astonishingly easy to talk to. She seemed to
understand just how he felt – sometimes she
even finished his sentences for him. Before
long, he was telling her all about his helpless,
hopeless love for Olivia.

'So, there you are,' he said finally. 'Now you know everything. I'm lost. I've never felt this way before.' He gazed beseechingly at Viola. 'But you can help me, I know you can. There's something about you – you're different from the other fellows. She'd listen to you, I'm sure she would. Go and see her for me – make her understand. Make her love me!'

'She probably won't even let me into the house,' Viola pointed out, thinking what an extraordinary colour the duke's eyes were.

'Make her. Do whatever it takes. Stick your foot in the door and refuse to move till you've seen her. You're just a boy, she won't see you as a threat. You have a sort of way about you...' He looked at her, puzzled for a moment, then gave her a brilliant smile. 'You won't regret it, I promise – you can have whatever you want if you pull this off for me – anything, anything at all!'

Viola gazed up at the duke. He was so tall, so stunningly, mouth-wateringly gorgeous.

21

'Can I really?' she said wistfully.

'Of course – anything!'

She watched as he walked away. And under her breath, she muttered, 'Then marry me. Not Olivia – me!'

But it wasn't going to happen, and she had a job to do. Viola sighed, and set off to do her duty.

Act Two

Olivia's household, it appeared, was very strange. The first person Viola saw was quite clearly drunk, even though it was only morning.

'What are you, sir?' he said to Viola, frowning and swaying slightly.

'What am I? Er … a gentleman, sir. Here to see…'

'Are you? Are you really a gentleman? Well in that case, she certainly won't see you!'

'Please tell the Lady Olivia that I must speak with her,' said Viola firmly.

'Oh, very well. But you're wasting your time, young man, you mark my words…'

The man tottered off and, minutes later, someone new appeared at the door. This person looked extremely sober. In fact, he looked as if he'd never touched a drink in his life. He stood as stiff as a poker and looked all the way down his extremely long nose at her.

'I am Malvolio, the Lady Olivia's steward,' he said.

'And I am Cesario, in the service of Duke Orsino, and I must speak with your lady.'

He sniffed disapprovingly. 'She is sick.'

'Then I will make her better.'

'She is weary.'

'She won't be once she hears what I have to say.'

He glared at her. 'Are you deaf? Listen very carefully – SHE WILL NOT SEE YOU!'

Viola folded her arms, looked him straight in the eye, and said calmly, 'Well, here's something for you to think about. I'M NOT MOVING UNTIL SHE DOES!'

Malvolio withdrew, slamming the door shut in her face. But in a few minutes he was back. 'My lady says she will see you,' he announced with obvious disapproval. 'Just for a moment. Follow me.'

'Ha!' thought Viola triumphantly. 'So far, so good!'

Now that she'd made it into the household, she was very curious to see what was so special about Olivia. 'She'd better be beautiful,' she thought to herself. 'And she'd better be good enough for him.'

But Olivia's face was hidden by a veil. It was impossible to have any idea what she looked like, or what kind of person she was.

Viola cleared her throat and swept a deep and very graceful bow.

'Most radiant, exquisite and unmatchable beauty...' She paused. 'Actually, before I carry on, I'd better check – you definitely are the Lady Olivia, aren't you? I mean, this is a good speech. I don't want to waste it on the wrong person.'

'Are you trying to be funny?' demanded Olivia.

'Oh no, not at all. I wouldn't dream of it. Well ... I'll just get on with the speech, shall I? I've spent ages on it. It's really very good...'

'Forget the speech,' snapped Olivia. 'Just say what you've come to say and let's get it over with.'

Viola glanced round at Olivia's attendants and leaned forward confidentially. 'It's private,' she said, her voice soft as a caress, her dark eyelashes fluttering. 'Not for the ears of others. You'll love it, I promise.'

Olivia was still for a moment. 'Very well,' she said, her voice a little husky. She dismissed her attendants, and then turned to Viola. 'There now. We are alone. You may begin.'

'Most sweet lady...'

'A good start. Now ... who have you come from?'

Viola hesitated. She knew this wouldn't go down well. 'I come from Orsino, madam,' she said.

'Oh,' said Olivia flatly.

'Yes. Madam, I'm sorry, but I must ask you again – please let me see your face. It's very difficult talking to someone when you can't see what they're thinking!'

'Did your master ask you to say that? It won't do him much good – he's not even here to see it. Oh, very well, I'll draw the curtain for you.' With a graceful gesture, she pushed back her veil. 'There,' she said. 'What do you think of the picture?'

Viola looked. Attractive enough, she thought to herself, if you like that sort of thing. Aloud, she said, 'It's excellently done, if God did all.'

Olivia looked a little put out. 'Well, of course he did. This is me, just as nature intended. What are you implying?'

'Nothing, nothing,' said Viola hastily, remembering why she was there. 'But how sad it would be, if you were to die and leave no child behind to carry on your beauty! Surely you wouldn't be that cruel to the world?'

'I wouldn't dream of it. I'll make a list, for the benefit of all those I leave behind. Two lips, indifferent grey, two grey eyes with lids to them, one chin, small, one neck, long...' Her fingers moved slowly downwards. 'And so forth...'

'Quite,' said Viola hastily. 'My lady, you are too cruel. But beautiful, undoubtedly. I must tell you, though, that my lord's love for you is so great that only the most beautiful woman in the whole world – which would be you, of course – could be worthy of it.'

'Go on,' purred Olivia. 'Tell me more!'

'He adores you,' floundered Viola. 'All he does is sigh and groan and weep, for love of you.'

'But you see – I'm not interested in your master. I've told him that. Can't he take no for an answer?'

Viola was beginning to get cross. Who did Olivia think she was?

'If I loved you as my master does,' she said passionately, 'I wouldn't find any sense in your attitude, either.'

'Oh?' Olivia lifted an elegantly arched eyebrow. 'And what would you do?'

Viola was silent for a moment. She thought how she felt about Orsino, and what she would do to make him love her. 'I'd weave a shelter from willow at your gate,' she said slowly.

'And I'd write beautiful songs to tell you how I feel. I'd sing them all through the night and all through the day. The hills and the sky would ring with your name, and you would hear nothing but that sweet sound. Then you'd understand – you'd soften, and in the end you'd surely take pity on me.'

Olivia was enchanted by his words. 'Who are you?' she whispered.

'Just a gentleman,' said Viola firmly.

Olivia collected herself. 'Well, you can go back to your lord and tell him that I can't love him, and there's no point in him sending any more messages. Only…' She hesitated. 'Only … you might come back again, just to tell me how he takes it. Oh … and here's a little something for your pains.'

Viola stared at the gold coin. 'You don't need to pay me,' she said coldly. 'Keep your money. It's my master who deserves a reward, not me.' She stood up, and looked down at Olivia. 'One day, I hope you'll know what it's like to love and not be loved in return. Farewell, fair cruelty.'

She stalked out, leaving Olivia to gaze after her in astonishment. 'Hm...' she thought to herself. 'Now if only you were pleading for yourself, you might get an altogether different answer.'

Malvolio came in, and she sat up and pulled a ring from her finger. 'Malvolio,' she said carelessly, 'that young man who was here just now – he gave me this ring, from his master, the duke. Tell him I'm not going to keep it. He must tell Orsino I'm not for him, and if he wants to know the reasons why, he must come back tomorrow. The young man, not the duke,' she added, just to be clear.

'Madam, I will,' said Malvolio with a bow.

After he'd gone, Olivia put her hands on her hot cheeks. 'What am I doing?' she whispered. 'I don't know anything about him. But ... it's fate. I can't do anything about it. What must be, will be.'

Only a few miles up the coast, on the very same morning that Viola had become a boy and first set eyes on Orsino, her brother Sebastian had also wept for the loss of a twin. His rescuer was a man named Antonio, who had seen the shipwreck from where he lived further up the coast, and searched the shore for survivors. He found Sebastian, battered by waves and injured by rocks, and nursed him in his cottage by the seashore. Sebastian was very weak, and his recovery was slow. But as he grew stronger, he began to think about finding his way home.

'I will go into the city,' he said. 'Antonio, you have been kindness itself – will you do one more thing for me, and show me the way?'

Antonio shook his head. 'I dare not be seen in Illyria,' he said.

Puzzled, Sebastian asked why.

'I was a sea captain and my ship was wrecked,' explained Antonio. 'I recently fought against Orsino, the Duke of Illyria. I sank two of his ships, but my own was damaged in the battle. Naturally, Orsino sees me as an enemy.'

'Did you kill many of his people?'

'No, but after the battle, when peace was made, the others on my side returned their plunder as part of the agreement. I refused.'

'I see,' said Sebastian. He was thoughtful for a while. 'Well then, I can never repay you for what you've done, but now I must say goodbye.'

Antonio frowned. 'I wish I could help you,' he said. 'But I cannot – it's as much as my life's worth.'

'Of course not,' said Sebastian warmly. 'You've done more than enough to help me already. I'd feel terrible if you came to harm because of me. No, my friend, I'll go alone. Don't worry – I'll be all right.'

They said goodbye, and Sebastian set off towards the town. Antonio hesitated. Sebastian was only a boy. What if he ran into robbers on the road? Not that he had any money – but they wouldn't know that. No, it was no good. He would only worry about him. Antonio put on a cloak with a hood and went after Sebastian.

'I'll keep my eyes open, and my hood up,' Antonio told him firmly. 'I won't risk going into the centre. But you've not been back on your feet for long – I can't let you go alone, and that's all there is to it.'

Sebastian smiled. 'Well … if you're sure. I must say, I'll be glad to have you along!'

When they reached the town, Antonio said he would keep to the outskirts, as they'd agreed. 'But here,' he said, 'take my purse, in case you see something you want to buy. I'll meet you later, at the Elephant – it's a good inn, to the south of the city. Anyone will tell you where to find it.'

Malvolio clutched his side. He had a terrible stitch. He shouldn't have to go running after people at his age. It was undignified, not to mention exhausting. He'd probably have a seizure, and then Olivia would be sorry.

At last, he caught up with Cesario. The insolent young puppy stared at him curiously.

Malvolio held out the ring. 'The Lady Olivia bids me return this ring to you. She says...' He paused and mopped his forehead with his handkerchief. 'She says to assure your master that she is not – and never will be – interested in him as a suitor, and that he needn't bother sending you again – unless it's just to tell her what he says. Tomorrow.'

Then he bowed stiffly, and turned to limp back to the house.

Viola stared at the ring, puzzled. She'd never seen it before. What was going on? An unwelcome thought struck her. 'Oh no! Don't say she's fallen for me! She did stare at me a lot. Oh dear. Oh very dear. He loves her, I love him, she loves me, and I'm really a girl. This is too hard a knot for me to untie!'

And, shaking her head in confusion, she set off back to the duke.

Act Three

That night, Sir Toby, Sir Andrew and Feste the clown woke the whole house again with their drinking and singing. First Maria came to scold them, and then Malvolio arrived.

'Are you quite mad?' he fumed. 'You should be ashamed of yourselves! My lady won't put up with this appalling carry-on for another minute. If you won't behave, you must leave.'

Sir Toby peered blearily at Malvolio. 'And who do you think you're talking to? You're nothing but a steward – a servant! Be off with you, you silly man. More wine, Maria!'

Malvolio glared at Maria, who was trying to hide a grin. 'What are you smiling at? Why, you're positively encouraging them! I don't like your attitude, and I'll be telling my lady all about it, make no mistake.'

He bustled off.

'Pompous twit,' muttered Sir Toby. 'I really can't stand the man.'

Maria nodded thoughtfully. She didn't appreciate being told off by Malvolio. 'He thinks far too much of himself,' she said. 'He needs to be taken down a peg – and I know just the way to do it...'

The next day, Orsino was still trying to cheer himself up by singing sad songs. He sighed heavily.

'You see what a faithful lover I am, Cesario? All I can think about is her. She takes up my thoughts in the day and my dreams at night. But what about you? Have you ever been in love?'

'Well ... perhaps a little, my lord.'

'I knew it! What's she like?'

'Rather like you, my lord.'

'Poor woman. How old is she?'

'About your age, my lord.'

'Well, that won't do. You need a woman who's younger than you. They don't keep their looks, you know, and we men are fickle creatures.'

'How true,' said Viola sadly. 'How true.'

There were more songs, and then Orsino dismissed everyone except Viola.

'Cesario,' he said seriously, 'you must go back to Olivia. She liked you, didn't she? You must try again for me.'

'But what if she really can't love you, my lord?' pleaded Viola. 'Imagine if there was a woman who really loved you, but you couldn't love her and you told her so. Wouldn't you expect her to accept your decision?'

'There's no comparison between a woman's love and a man's,' said the duke. 'Men feel things far more strongly.'

Viola plunged on. 'Oh? Well, my father had a daughter who loved a man. Just as, if I were a woman, I might love you.'

Their eyes locked. Orsino was puzzled. 'Go on,' he said slowly. 'What happened to this sister of yours?'

'She ... she pined away. Because the man didn't love her back. I'm the only one of my family left now. Well, I think so, anyway.'

Viola looked away and cleared her throat. 'Must I go to the countess, then, my lord?'

'Yes. Give her this jewel. Say ... say I won't take no for an answer.'

Viola bowed, and set off for Olivia's house, with Orsino gazing thoughtfully after her. There was something strange about Cesario – something strange, but oddly attractive...

Maria had found Sir Toby, Sir Andrew and Fabian, who was another gentleman of Olivia's household. She had come up with a plan to make a fool of Malvolio, and she couldn't wait to tell them all about it.

'Quick,' she said, 'Malvolio's heading this way – we haven't got much time. I've written some letters to him – look, don't you think the writing is exactly like my lady's? It's good enough to fool him, anyway. He's already had two, and I'll leave this one here on the bench, ready for him to find. Oh, this is going to be such fun!'

'But what's in them?' asked Sir Toby.

'Well ... oh, look, he's coming! No time to explain – you'll soon see. Quick, get behind the hedge.'

The hedge was made of box, which was clipped into the shape of clubs, hearts, diamonds and spades, so there were plenty of useful nooks and crannies for the plotters to peer through. Soon, Malvolio approached, strolling down the path and talking to himself. When they heard what he was saying, Sir Toby and the others could hardly contain themselves.

'Clearly, it's destiny; after all, why shouldn't Olivia fall in love with me? I'm a fine-looking fellow, and she's always treated me with the very greatest of respect. Oh, I can just see how it will be when we're married... I'll leave her lounging in bed, and then I'll summon our relative, cousin Toby, and tell him he must give up his drinking – oh, and he must get rid of that ninny of a friend of his, Sir Andrew... Now, what's this? Another letter! Why, the dear little minx – she must have left it here, knowing I'd find it. Now, let me see...'

'Oh, please let him read it out loud,' muttered Fabian.

'Shh!' whispered Sir Toby.

'Yes, it's her seal... *I may command where I adore...* There! What could be clearer? She loves me! *Be not afraid of greatness. Some are born great, some achieve greatness, and some have greatness thrust upon them.* How true, how true. *Be opposite with a kinsman, surly with servants...* No problem there, no problem at all. *...and remember how much I liked your yellow stockings and cross garters.* Funny, I didn't think she did – but ladies are so changeable, bless them. I'll wear them every single day. And what's this bit at the end? *If you love me, my sweet, smile for me.* For you, my love – anything!'

Clutching the letter to his heart, Malvolio hurried off, and the plotters all came out of their hiding places, spluttering with laughter.

'Oh, Maria, Maria, it's too good!' said Sir Toby, wiping his eyes.

'Can't you just see it?' said Maria gleefully. 'He's going to get himself up in yellow stockings and cross garters – which she absolutely hates – and he'll be simpering and grinning, when she just wants to be miserable. Oh, I could almost feel sorry for him!'

'But not quite,' said Sir Andrew. 'Did you hear what he called me? A ninny! What cheek!'

'Most unfair,' said Fabian hastily.

'Come on,' urged Maria. 'Let's go after him. This is going to be too good to miss.'

Olivia dismissed her servants, saying she would walk with Cesario in the orchard. Then she turned to Viola with a brilliant smile. Viola groaned inwardly. It was written all over Olivia's face: she was in love with him. Her. Them.

'Give me your hand, sir,' said Olivia.

Viola bowed politely. 'Your servant, princess,' she said.

'My servant? Oh no, I don't think so. Surely you are Orsino's servant!' said Olivia playfully.

'But Orsino is your servant – completely yours, totally at your service – so I am your servant's servant. So, *yours* by definition, because all a servant has belongs to his master. Or mistress.' Viola added, beginning to feel slightly confused.

Olivia tossed her head impatiently. 'Oh, Orsino! He's such a bore – I don't want to hear about him, I've already told you that.' She moved closer. 'I'd much rather hear about you.'

Viola gulped. 'Dear lady...'

'No, not another word. Now ... when we last met, I sent my man after you with a ring. I'm sorry, it must have been awkward for you – I said it was yours, and of course it wasn't. I put myself completely at your mercy. Now, tell me – what did you think? Were you surprised? What did you feel? Did you feel anything? The truth, now – you can be honest!'

Viola stared at Olivia. She looked so

vulnerable, so eager. And Viola had no choice but to hurt her.

'I'm so sorry,' she said quietly. 'I pity you, I really do. But that's all.'

It was enough. Olivia was quiet for a moment. Then she raised her head and put on a brave smile. 'Well, if I had to be hurt, I'm glad it was by you. Don't worry, I won't make things difficult for you. One day, when you're older, you'll find a wife to love, and she'll be a lucky woman. Now ... I think you'd better go.'

Viola hesitated. 'You won't say anything to the duke, madam?'

Olivia shook her head. 'No, but before you go, please... I would just like to know how you think of me now.'

'I think ... that you think you're not what you are.'

Olivia smiled sadly. 'And I think much the same of you.'

'It's true,' said Viola. 'I'm not what I seem to be.'

'I wish you were how I'd like you to be.'

'Would that be better? Perhaps. In any case, I swear this: my heart is my own, and no woman shall ever be mistress of it. So, farewell, madam; I will never speak for my master to you again.'

'You shouldn't give up,' said Olivia, making just one more try. 'Come again. Who knows? Perhaps you might be able to persuade me in favour of the duke after all.'

But, as she watched him go, Olivia was more certain than ever that it was not the master she loved, but the servant.

They'd thought they were alone, but they were wrong. Sir Andrew had been spying on them. He was too far away to hear what they said, but it was obvious from their body language what was happening.

'I won't stay a minute longer,' he huffed to Sir Toby and Fabian. 'She's more interested in the duke's serving man than she is in me.

You should have seen them just now in the orchard – it was quite disgraceful.'

Fabian shook his head. 'No, no, no, Sir Andrew. You've got it all wrong, really you have. She wants you to fight for her, that's what it is. That'll show her you really care.'

Sir Andrew looked doubtful. 'Do you think so?'

'There's no doubt about it,' agreed Sir Toby. 'Challenge the boy to a duel. Go and write it down, and I'll deliver it.'

'Sir Andrew's a very dear friend of yours, isn't he?' said Fabian, after Sir Andrew had bustled off.

Sir Toby shrugged. 'Of course he is. He has plenty of money and I have none. It's a match made in heaven.'

'So you wouldn't actually deliver a challenge?'

'Yes, I would. But there's no danger it'll come to a fight. They're both afraid of their own shadows. Oh, here's Maria. What news, Maria? What's going on?'

'Come quickly,' she crowed, 'Malvolio's all set, with yellow stockings, cross garters and smiles all over his silly face. Oh, my lady's going to be furious!'

Olivia had not given up on Cesario. She'd sent him a message, and was waiting for his reply. Feeling agitated, she summoned Malvolio. He seemed to be the only one in her household with any sense at the moment, and she felt he would suit her mood.

But when she saw him, she could hardly believe her eyes. His usually serious face was covered with smiles – and what had he got on his legs? Yellow stockings and cross garters, which he knew she hated! What on earth had come over him?

'You must be ill, Malvolio – you must go to bed at once,' she ordered.

He leered horribly. 'If you say so, sweetheart,' he drawled, and blew her a kiss.

'Malvolio, what can you be thinking of?'

scolded Maria. 'Are you mad?'

He winked, and struck a pose. '*Be not afraid of greatness* – a true word indeed…'

'What did you say, Malvolio?' said Olivia, bewildered.

'*Some are born great…*'

'I beg your pardon?'

'*Some achieve greatness…*'

'Oh, enough!'

'*And some have greatness thrust upon them,* eh?'

At this point, a servant entered and murmured that Orsino's servant had been reluctantly persuaded to return. Olivia turned to Maria. 'Something must be done about Malvolio – he's taken leave of his senses. Find my cousin Toby, and ask him to take care of him. I must go and see Cesario. I … er … I expect he has another message from the duke.'

'There you are!' said Malvolio triumphantly to himself. 'She has asked her own cousin to take care of me. It's just as she said in the letter;

she's giving me an opportunity to put him in his place. *Be opposite with a kinsman* she said. Oh, and here he is, and Fabian, too. I'm going to enjoy this…'

'How are you, my dear fellow?' enquired Sir Toby tenderly.

'Not to put to fine a point on it, I've nothing to say to you,' declared Malvolio. 'Go away. Go on – shoo.'

'My lady wants you to take care of him,' Maria told Sir Toby.

'Does she indeed?' said Malvolio, with a mocking smile.

'Come now, Malvolio,' said Sir Toby. 'What are you thinking of, behaving like this?'

'Oh, go hang yourselves,' retorted Malvolio. 'I haven't got time to waste on the likes of you.'

The plotters watched him gleefully as he wandered off towards the house, picking a rose and smelling it with evident delight.

'Our work is not yet done,' said Fabian.

'No, indeed. What do you say we lock him

up in a nice dark cellar to cool off?' suggested Sir Toby. 'Just for his own good, of course.'

Maria nodded. 'It would be for the best,' she said solemnly. 'And think how quiet it will be without him.'

Sir Andrew appeared next, walking slowly along the garden path. He had a piece of parchment in his hand, and was looking at it closely.

'Oh, here's more fun,' said Fabian. 'Sir Andrew with his challenge.'

'Listen to this,' said Sir Andrew. 'It's very good.'

'Yes, yes, of course, my dear fellow,' said Sir Toby. 'We'll have a look at it presently. Meanwhile, you can go and wait in the orchard. Cesario is in with Olivia now. You can lie in wait for him, and when he leaves, you can jump out and scare him. Draw your sword, scowl horribly, that sort of thing.'

'Right,' said Sir Andrew. 'Yes. Draw my sword, you say? I'll see what I can do.'

'He's pathetic, isn't he?' said Fabian cheerfully, watching as Sir Andrew swaggered off.

Sir Toby nodded, looking at the challenge. 'This wouldn't scare a mouse. I'll make something up instead. And I'll tell Cesario that Sir Andrew's a brilliant fighter, never been beaten, that kind of thing. Oh, they'll be so scared of each other they'll be quivering wrecks! Look – here's the boy now, with my niece. Come on, let's make ourselves scarce, then I'll nab him as soon as he's alone.'

'You have a heart of stone,' Olivia was saying reproachfully. 'I've said far too much. I try to stop myself, but I just can't help it.'

'My master feels the same,' said Viola loyally. 'He's twice as miserable as you are, at least.'

Olivia ignored this. 'Please – wear this for me.' It was a locket, containing a miniature portrait of her. 'Unlike me, it can't speak, so it shouldn't get on your nerves too much. And come again tomorrow.' She put her hand on Viola's sleeve and gazed at her, tears trembling in her eyes. 'Remember – I can deny you nothing!'

'Then I ask you this,' pleaded Viola. 'Please, please, give your love to Orsino.'

Olivia snatched her hand away, and cried out in frustration, 'Anything but that! Oh, how can you be so cruel?' Then, sobbing, she turned on her heel and ran back to the house.

Act Four

Viola sighed. What a mess it all was! Dejectedly, she set off to make her report to the duke.

'Young sir – hello there! A word, if you please!'

Viola turned. It was Olivia's cousin, the usually drunken Sir Toby, together with his friend Fabian. 'Yes?' she said politely.

'I just wanted to warn you,' puffed the portly knight. 'I don't know what you've done to him, but you've got an enemy lying in wait for you on the other side of the orchard. He's breathing fire, I tell you – he's really very cross!'

Viola was bewildered. 'Oh, I'm sure you must be mistaken. I haven't made an enemy of anyone, I'm sure I haven't.'

'Oh yes, you have. And, what's more, he's big and strong and extremely fierce.'

Viola began to panic. 'Who is this man?'

'He's a knight, fierce and brave. He's a real killer, and he's so angry he says nothing less than your death will satisfy him.'

Viola thought fast. 'I'll go back to the house and ask for protection.'

'No, I'm sorry, honour won't allow it. The knight deserves to be answered, and now you must give him satisfaction. Surely you aren't afraid?'

'But I haven't done anything to him! I don't even know him! Please, sir – could you find out what this is all about?'

'Well, I suppose I could try. But I'm not making any promises. Fabian, you wait here with Cesario.'

Anxiously, Viola asked Fabian to tell her what he knew.

'Only that the knight is well and truly furious with you. And that he's the best fighter in Illyria. I'd be worried if I were you – very worried.'

'Oh dear!' said Viola. What on earth was she to do? If she had to fight Sir Andrew, for one thing everyone would realise she was a fraud, and for another, she'd probably die, so she didn't need Fabian to tell her she should be worried.

'You'll have to go and meet him, you know. Come along – perhaps I can persuade him to make peace with you.'

'Oh yes, please! I'm no fighter, and I don't care who knows it.'

Meanwhile, Sir Toby was terrifying Sir Andrew with tales of what a skilled swordsman Cesario was.

'I'll have to back out! I can't take on someone like that,' spluttered Sir Andrew.

'Oh nonsense, you'll be fine. Anyway, you've no choice – he's all fired up now, and he's on his way.'

'Tell him he can have my horse – it's a marvellous horse, he'll love it. Tell him anything – just get me out of it!'

Sir Toby sighed and shook his head. 'Well, I'll see what I can do. But no promises, mind.' And he hurried off to find Viola.

She was looking pale and anxious.

'I'm afraid Sir Andrew feels he cannot withdraw,' he told her. 'He is an honourable man, you see. What would people think of him? But he's promised not to hurt you.'

Viola felt sick with fear. But there was no way out. She trailed after Sir Toby – who meanwhile was telling Sir Andrew exactly the same tale.

The intrepid heroes finally came face to face in the street in front of Olivia's house. Both trembling like leaves, they drew their swords.

Then, suddenly, a complete stranger appeared on the scene. Flourishing his sword, he leapt in front of Viola and ordered Sir Andrew to back off.

'Who the devil are you?' asked Sir Toby, peering at the new arrival in astonishment.

'My name is Antonio, friend to this young man here, and determined to defend him to the death!'

'Oh,' said Sir Toby, drawing his own sword. 'Well, in that case, you'll have to answer to me.'

'Sir Toby, stop!' said Fabian urgently. 'Look

– officers of the law!'

Two sergeants appeared on the scene.

'Put up your swords, all of you!' ordered one of them.

'This isn't over,' growled Sir Toby to Antonio.

Viola appealed to Sir Andrew. 'Sir, do please put up your sword.'

'Certainly, certainly,' said Sir Andrew, pushing his sword hastily back into its scabbard. 'And, by the way, I'll be as good as my word. It's a very good horse – I'm sure you'll be pleased.'

Viola stared at him, bewildered. What on earth was he talking about?

Meanwhile, the mysterious stranger was trying to persuade the officers not to arrest him. 'You're mistaking me for someone else,' he pleaded.

'Not at all,' retorted the sergeant. 'I know perfectly well who you are. You're an enemy of Illyria, and the duke will be delighted to see you – in chains! Take him away, boys.'

Antonio turned to Viola. 'Alas! The game's up. I don't regret what I've done, but I'm afraid I must ask you to give me back what's left of the money. As you see. I'm going to need it.'

'What money, sir?' Viola was now thoroughly confused. 'I'm very grateful for what you did, and I'll gladly lend you half of what I have, but I'm afraid that doesn't amount to very much.'

Antonio couldn't believe it. How could Sebastian be so ungrateful? After all he'd done!

'Come along, sir,' said the sergeant grimly.

'Wait ... wait just a minute! How can this be? Sebastian, I saved your life, I cared for you – is this how you're going to reward me? Have you no shame?'

'Oh, you're breaking my heart, you really are,' said the sergeant. 'Come along now – time to go. There's a nice comfy dungeon waiting for you.'

Viola watched them leave. She was beginning to understand. 'He really believes it,' she said to herself. 'He thinks I'm Sebastian. Does this mean what I think it does? Could it possibly be that my brother is still alive?' In a dream, she began to walk back to Orsino's.

Sir Toby was disapproving. 'Did you see that? What a coward. And fancy letting his friend down like that. Very bad form.'

'Definitely a coward,' agreed Fabian.

'I'll go after him,' blustered Sir Andrew. 'I'll beat him within an inch of his life – I'll teach him not to mess with me!'

Chuckling, Sir Toby and Fabian followed to see the fun.

'Let me get this right,' said Feste, as he and Sebastian stood in the street near Olivia's house. 'Are you trying to tell me you're not the person I've been sent to fetch?'

Sebastian stared at him in astonishment. Was the man mad? 'I don't know who lives in this house, and I've never met you before in my life.'

Feste bristled. 'And I suppose I don't know

you, and my lady didn't send me to speak to you, and your name's not Master Cesario – and this here isn't my nose!' he said, touching it. 'In fact, nothing that is so is so!'

Sebastian was beginning to feel annoyed. 'Look, why don't you just clear off? You've obviously mistaken me for someone else.'

'Oh, is that a fact?' sneered Feste. 'Right – well I'll just go back in and tell my lady then, and see what she has to say about it!'

At this moment, Sir Andrew, Sir Toby and Fabian arrived. Sir Andrew swaggered up to Sebastian, putting up his fists. 'Ha! Got you! Here – take this!' And he punched him hard.

Sebastian promptly put up his own fists. 'What is going on? You're all completely mad! Take this then – and this!'

'Stop!' said Sir Toby, grabbing Sebastian's arm. 'Leave him alone!'

'I'll have the law on him, the scoundrel!' huffed Sir Andrew.

'Let me go!' roared Sebastian.

'Certainly not,' said Sir Toby. 'You need to calm down, young man.'

'I said, let me go!' And with that, Sebastian shook off Sir Toby and drew his sword. Not to be outdone, Sir Toby drew his, and they began to circle round each other warily.

Suddenly the door to Olivia's house was flung open and she appeared, looking furious. 'Toby! How dare you? Put up your sword this instant, and get out of my sight! Go on – go! Cesario, I'm so sorry – please come inside. My stupid cousin's always causing trouble, I don't know why I put up with it. Just because he is my cousin, I suppose… I hope you can forgive him.'

Sebastian was now completely bewildered. This woman appeared to be mad, too. But she was also very beautiful, and he allowed her to persuade him to go inside.

'Come now,' she was saying. 'I wish you'd do as I say.'

'Oh,' he said, looking at her admiringly, 'I will!'

She looked at him, startled. Cesario seemed to have changed his tune. 'Well … good!' she murmured.

A little later, not content with just locking Malvolio up, Maria, Feste and Sir Toby were discussing plans to torment him further. Feste dressed up in a clerical robe and a false beard to look like a priest they knew called Sir Topas, and they went to see the prisoner.

Malvolio begged the so-called priest to go to Olivia for him, and ask her to release him from this hideous darkness.

'Darkness? Why, you poor lunatic, this room is as bright as day! You're possessed by the devil – it's quite clear that you are. You must stay here, I'm afraid.'

'But can't you see – I'm no more mad than you are!' said poor Malvolio.

It was all great fun, but Sir Toby knew it couldn't go on much longer. 'My niece is really cross with me,' he said to Feste after they'd left the miserable steward. 'I'd love to carry on with this, but if she finds out what we've been up to, I think that'll be it. She'll throw me out, and then what will I do? Feste, you'd better go and see him again, just as yourself. We'd better wind it up.'

And, regretfully, after just a little more teasing, Feste agreed to fetch light, ink and paper, so that Malvolio could write and explain himself to Olivia.

While Malvolio was shut in darkness, unable to understand how he'd been brought so low, Sebastian, equally confused, was outside in the sunshine contemplating his good fortune. Olivia had presented him with a beautiful pearl, and made it very clear that she was desperately in love with him – yet he'd only just met her. He shook his head in puzzlement. He wondered where Antonio was. Antonio was older and more experienced; Sebastian had come to rely on his advice. Could Olivia be mad? She didn't seem mad. And how could she manage her house and servants so well if she was? No, it didn't make sense. Nothing made sense. There was definitely more to all this than met the eye. Ah – here she was. And with ... a priest? Her eyes were shining with excitement. How lovely she was! She took his hand.

'If you love me, my precious, come with me now, and this priest shall marry us in secret. We needn't tell anyone until you're ready, but I would feel so much better if I knew you were really mine in the sight of God. Will you do this for me?'

How could he refuse her? Actually, he didn't even want to. He kissed her hand. 'I will. I'll go with you and, having sworn truth, ever will be true.'

Olivia closed her eyes and sighed with happiness. At last!

Act Five

'Oh, come on, Feste,' wheedled Fabian. 'Show me Malvolio's letter. Just a little look – go on, you know you want to!'

'Certainly not,' said Feste severely. 'It wouldn't be right. Now, who have we got here?'

It was Orsino, with Viola and some of his gentlemen. He recognised Feste and asked him to go and tell Olivia that he wished to speak with her.

Orsino waited impatiently for a reply. Would she see him this time? He didn't know what he was going to do if she wouldn't. He sighed, flicking a speck of dust from his sleeve. Women were very strange, he thought gloomily. After all, he was quite good looking, or so he'd always had reason to believe. He was witty, wealthy, a wise ruler – but not so wise when it came to love, obviously.

There was a commotion along the street, two officers with a prisoner stumbling between them. Orsino's eyes narrowed. There was something familiar about this man...

'Why, sir,' said Viola. 'That's the man I was telling you about – the one who rescued me from the madman!'

'I know him, too,' said Orsino, suddenly placing him. 'He was the captain of a ship that fought against my fleet. He's an enemy of Illyria.'

One of the officers nodded. 'It's him, right enough, sir. It was when he boarded the *Tiger* that your nephew lost his leg, if you remember.'

'Of course I do – how could I forget? What on earth has possessed him to show his face here?'

Viola stood up for Antonio. 'He was kind to me, sir – he drew his sword to defend me. But he said some strange things – I didn't quite know what to make of it.'

Orsino stared coldly at Antonio. 'You're a pirate and a thief and you've put yourself among enemies. Would you care to explain why?'

Antonio met his gaze. 'I may be your enemy, but I'm neither a thief nor a pirate and I never have been. As for why I'm here – you may well ask.' He paused, and glanced bitterly at Viola. 'I rescued that boy there from the sea three months ago. He was close to death, and I nursed him back to health – he said himself that I had given him back his life. He wanted to come into the city, and against my better judgement, I came, too. I defended him when he was attacked, and that's when I was taken. And then – I can hardly believe it even now – he refused to give me back the money I'd lent him and, worse than that, he denied he even knew me!'

Viola shook her head in bewilderment. 'But I don't – I've never seen you before, I swear it!'

'When did he come to this town?' asked Orsino crisply.

'Today, my lord. Before that we were together for three months, ever since I rescued him from the sea.'

Orsino glanced away. The door was opening, to reveal Olivia with her attendants. His gaze softened.

'Now heaven walks on earth ... but as for you, villain, you are speaking nonsense. This youth has been in my service for three months.' He gestured to the officers. 'Wait here with him. I'll speak to him again later.'

Olivia smiled tenderly at Viola, then turned back to Orsino. 'What can I do for you, my lord? Aside from the obvious, of course... Cesario, where have you been? We arranged to meet!'

'What?' Viola stared at her, confused.

'Olivia...' interrupted Orsino.

'Cesario,' said Olivia, laying a hand on Viola's arm. 'What do you have to say to me?'

'My lord wishes to speak,' said Viola in confusion. 'It is my duty to be silent.'

Olivia stared at her, then turned to Orsino. 'Is it going to be the same old song? If so, I really don't want to hear it.'

'Still so cruel?' flashed back Orsino.

'Still so constant,' she retorted.

'Being constant in being cruel is nothing to

boast about,' he told her bitterly. 'I've been so faithful, so devoted – and all this seems to mean nothing to you. What am I to do?'

She shrugged. 'Whatever you like.'

For a moment, Orsino was silent, grappling with his emotions. Then he spoke. 'Whatever I like? Then perhaps I should kill you.' Everyone gasped, but Orsino ignored them. He had eyes only for Olivia. 'At least then, no one else would have you,' he went on. 'But I think I know – I think I see who it is you love instead of me. It's him, isn't it? Cesario. So perhaps I'll let you live – and kill him instead.' His eyes burned in his pale face. 'Yes, that's what I'll do. Come on, boy – I'll sacrifice the lamb that I do love, to spite a raven's heart within a dove.'

Viola gazed at him. 'If you asked it, I would die for you,' she said quietly. And, as if in a dream, she moved to follow him.

Distraught, Olivia cried, 'Where are you going, Cesario?'

'I'm going after the man I love, more than

these eyes – more than my life. More than I shall ever love a wife, as God is my witness.'

Olivia sank to her knees. 'He hates me! How I've been deceived!'

'Who has deceived you?' said Viola. 'What are you talking about?'

'Have you forgotten already?' cried Olivia passionately. 'Is this afternoon so long ago?' She turned to a servant. 'Go and fetch the priest!'

'Enough of this,' said Orsino impatiently. 'Come, Cesario.'

'Cesario – husband – stay!'

At that, everyone froze. Then, so slowly, Orsino turned to Olivia.

'Husband?'

'Yes, husband! See if he can deny it.'

Orsino looked at Viola. 'Well? Are you her … husband?'

'No! I swear it!'

Olivia shook her head. 'Oh, Cesario, I see what's happening here. You are afraid, and no wonder. But don't be. Be what you are – and then you'll be as great as the one you fear. Ah – here is the priest. Father, please, we had intended to keep it a secret, but the news is out. Please tell everyone what recently passed between this young man and myself.'

'Why – I married you, not two hours ago!'

Orsino was so angry that he could hardly speak. He turned on Viola in fury. 'You … you two-faced little so-and-so! Good grief, if you're like this now, what will you turn into when you're older? Go on – go with her. But I'll tell you one thing – you'd better be very sure you never cross my path again, or I won't be responsible for my actions.'

By now Viola was completely bewildered. She began to protest, but Olivia interrupted her. 'No, don't say another thing. And don't be frightened of him – he's just a bully!'

As if this wasn't enough, just then Sir Andrew came tottering along the street, with blood streaming from a cut on his head.

'For God's sake,' he gasped, 'find a doctor and send him to Sir Toby.'

'What's the matter?' asked Olivia, staring in astonishment. 'Whatever's happened?'

'We've been attacked! I've got one bloody head, and Sir Toby's got another. Oh, I wish I was at home!' lamented the miserable knight.

'Sir Andrew,' said Olivia firmly. 'Stop gibbering, and tell me who did this.'

'Why, the duke's man, Cesario! We thought he was a coward, but he's no such thing – he's the devil in person!'

'My Cesario?' said Orsino in disbelief.

Sir Andrew's gaze fell on Viola and his eyes widened. He took a step back. 'Oh no! He's here! Oh, don't hurt me – I never did a thing, it was all Sir Toby's idea.'

'But why are you saying this to me?' said Viola, flustered. 'I never hurt you. You drew your sword on me without cause – I never said a word out of place, and I certainly did you no harm.'

Sir Toby, supported by Feste, was the next to stagger onto the scene, as Sir Andrew replied, wagging his finger at Viola reproachfully.

'A bloody head – don't you call that a hurt? Now then ... here's poor Sir Toby. If he'd been sober, you wouldn't have got away with it, that's for sure.'

'Sir Toby – how are you?' asked Orsino.

Sir Toby waved him aside irritably. 'Oh, I'm all right. Just a cut, I can cope with that. Sir Andrew – I thought you were going to find a doctor?'

'Oh, the quack's been drunk since first thing this morning,' said Feste dismissively. 'You won't get much sense out of him.'

'Then he's a blasted idiot and a nuisance. If there's one thing I can't stand, it's a drunk.'

Olivia found her voice. 'Away with him. Who's at the bottom of all this?'

'I'll help you, Sir Toby,' said Sir Andrew kindly. 'Come along, lean on me. We'll get our wounds dressed together.'

But Sir Toby, feeling completely out of sorts, would have none of it. 'Help? You? You're a fool, man – a waste of good skin!'

Sir Andrew stared at him, appalled, and for a moment there was silence, which was eventually broken by Olivia.

'Get Sir Toby to bed,' she said. 'And find someone to look at his wound.'

And with that, Feste, Fabian, Sir Toby and Sir Andrew all stumbled off into the house.

And then someone else arrived. A young man, who looked remarkably like Cesario.

Olivia gasped, staring wildly at him.

'I'm sorry, madam, I really am,' he said, taking her hand and kissing it. 'I didn't want to hurt your cousin, but he honestly didn't leave me any choice. Oh dear, don't look at me like that – forgive me, for the sake of our vows!'

It was Sebastian.

Everyone's eyes travelled from him to Viola and back again. Orsino was the first to find his voice.

'One face, one voice, the same clothes – why, one's a mirror image of the other!'

Then Sebastian caught sight of Antonio, still under guard. Delighted, he said, 'Antonio, you're here! Thank goodness – I've been so worried about you!'

'Sebastian? Is it you?' said Antonio, staring as if he'd seen a ghost.

'Yes, of course it is,' said Sebastian.

'But...' Antonio looked at Viola and then back at Sebastian. 'How have you done this? Have you split yourself in two? Which of you is Sebastian?'

Olivia looked hugely pleased. 'Two of you! Fantastic,' she breathed, looking from one to the other.

Then Sebastian caught sight of Viola. 'Is that me standing there?' he said in disbelief. 'It can't be – I never had a brother. I had a sister, but she was drowned. Are you related to me? Where are you from? What's your name? Who are your parents?'

Viola gazed back at him, trembling slightly. 'I'm from Messalina. My father was called Sebastian, and so was my brother.' She reached out to touch his sleeve. 'He wore clothes just like these the last time I saw him, before our ship was wrecked and he was drowned. Are you – are you his ghost?'

'I'm just the same Sebastian I ever was,' said Sebastian gently. 'And if you were a woman, I'd give you a big hug, and I'd call you Viola.'

'My father had a mole on his forehead,' said Viola in a rush.

'Mine, too!'

'And he died on Viola's thirteenth birthday.'

'Yes, yes – I remember it well!'

He seized her hands. 'Oh, Viola! I can't believe it! Tell me everything – what happened to you after the shipwreck? And why are you dressed like this?'

A smile lit up Viola's face, and she said eagerly, 'I left my clothes with the captain of our ship – he lives in this town, and it was he who saved me. After that, I went into the service of the duke – and that was how I came to be caught up between him and the Lady Olivia.'

Sebastian turned to Olivia and took her hands. 'Now it all becomes clear! You're betrothed both to a man and a maid!'

Orsino hardly knew what to make of it, or what he should feel. Olivia was lost to him. But somehow he didn't feel too upset. If he was honest, he'd always felt strangely drawn to Cesario. In fact, a few minutes ago, when he'd thought he'd lost them both, he really couldn't have said whether he was more jealous of Olivia or Cesario.

He gazed at Viola. Then he touched her lips with a finger. 'So these ... are a woman's lips. How could I not have realised? And you've said a thousand times that you'd never love a woman as you loved me,' he remembered.

Her mouth twitched. 'Said it and meant it,' she said demurely.

Orsino took Viola's hand, turned it upside

down, and kissed her palm. 'Let me see you in your woman's clothes,' he murmured. 'I think we can safely say that from this time forward, you shall be your master's mistress.'

'Of course, my lord. Nothing would give me greater pleasure.'

So all was sunshine again – or almost all. There were still a few shadows left. Sir Andrew was saddened to realise that Sir Toby, whom he'd believed to be his friend, had in fact despised him all along. Sir Toby saw well enough that now his niece was married, she and her husband were unlikely to put up with his antics any longer. And Malvolio hated them all for having teased and tricked him.

But for Viola, Orsino, Sebastian and Olivia, love had triumphed, in spite of all the misunderstandings. And for them, that was all that truly mattered.

About the Author

Sue Purkiss was born in Derbyshire, read English at Durham University and taught the subject in Leicestershire and Somerset. More recently she has worked with young offenders, and for the last two years with students at Exeter University, where she has been a Royal Literary Fellow.

Her first book, *Spook School*, was published by A & C Black in 2003. Her most recent ones, *Warrior King* and *Emily's Surprising Voyage*, are historical fiction published by Walker.

She had a thoroughly enjoyable time writing *Twelfth Night*, which was the first Shakespeare play she ever saw, in a production at the school she went to in Ilkeston. Viola is definitely her favourite character, but she rather likes Antonio, too; he's obviously a good man to have around when times are hard!

William Shakespeare's

AS YOU LIKE IT

Retold by Jenny Oldfield

SHAKESPEARE TODAY

WILLIAM SHAKESPEARE'S

ROMEO & JULIET

RETOLD BY MICHAEL COX

WILLIAM
SHAKESPEARE'S

A Midsummer Night's Dream

RETOLD BY
ROBERT
SWINDELLS

SHAKESPEARE TODAY

WILLIAM SHAKESPEARE'S

The Tempest

RETOLD BY

FRANZESKA G. EWART

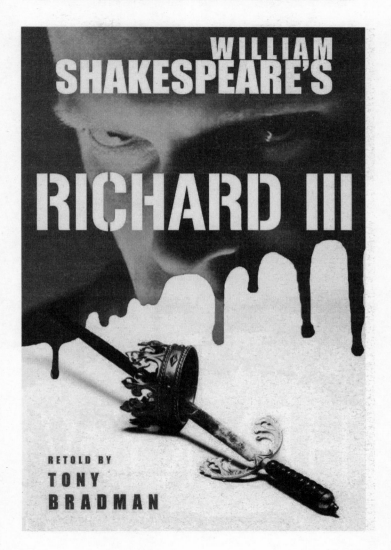

WILLIAM
SHAKESPEARE'S

RICHARD III

RETOLD BY
TONY
BRADMAN

SHAKESPEARE TODAY

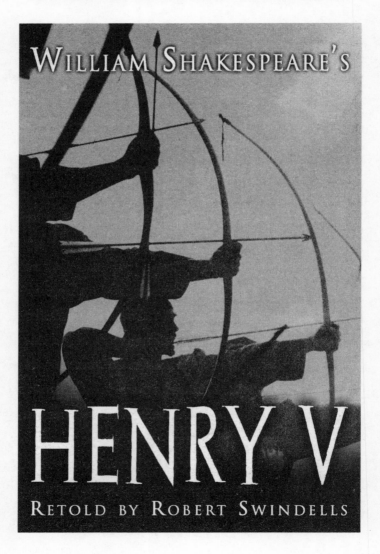

WILLIAM SHAKESPEARE'S

HENRY V

RETOLD BY ROBERT SWINDELLS

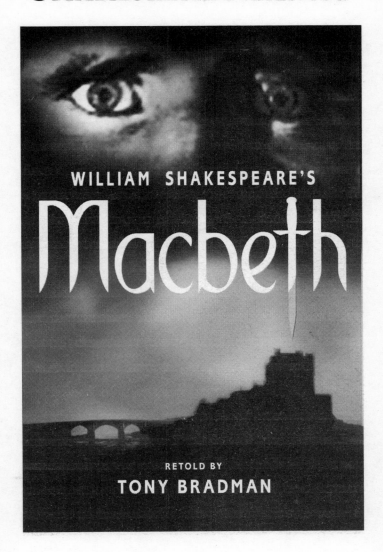

WILLIAM SHAKESPEARE'S

Macbeth

RETOLD BY

TONY BRADMAN

SHAKESPEARE TODAY

William Shakespeare's

Much Ado About Nothing

Retold by Jenny Oldfield